What Happened to Marion's Book?

By Brook Berg

Illustrations by Nathan Alberg

UpstartBooks

Fort Atkinson, Wisconsin

Published by UpstartBooks
W5527 Highway 106
P.O. Box 800
Fort Atkinson, Wisconsin 53538-0800
1-800-448-4887

Text © 2003 by Brook Berg
Illustrations © 2003 by Nathan Alberg

To my husband Harry and our children, Jonn and Miranda. I would not have taken the chance on Marion without your love and support.
To Beth who brought people to Marion's library and Liza who always believed.
And many thanks to Nathan, your illustrations have brought Marion to life!

Marion loves books, and she has all kinds. She has storybooks. She has joke books. She has picture books. She has poetry books. Marion even has books about animals and cars and places far away.

Marion gets books as gifts. She gets books for her birthday, and she gets books on holidays. And sometimes, when she is very, very good, she and Mommy go shopping at the big, big bookstore in the city!

Marion takes her books everywhere. She reads her books in the morning at the breakfast table. She takes her books outside when she plays. She reads in the car. Sometimes she even reads in the bathtub! And if she isn't too tired, she usually reads one more book right before bedtime.

Nana says that after Marion finishes school, she will surely grow up to be a librarian. Nana tells her that librarians help people find good books to read, and they read stories to kids who visit the library. "Marion the Librarian" has a nice ring to it, Marion thinks! She can hardly wait to go to school so that she can grow up to be a librarian!

At last, the big day arrives—Marion starts school! The first week, Marion learns many things. She learns to find her desk. She learns to wait her turn at the drinking fountain and in the lunch line. She learns where to find the playground, the music room, and the **library!**

Marion also learns that in her school, the library is called the Media Center, and that the librarian is named Mrs. Carlson. But the very best thing Marion learns is that she can check out two new books from the Media Center every week! So this is just what Marion does.

After school, Marion rushes home with her books. First she reads one book, and then the other. Later that evening, Mommy reads one book to her and Daddy reads the other. The next day, after school, Nana reads both books to her at least twice. Marion loves the stories.

At breakfast on Saturday morning, Marion brings her books to the table so that she can enjoy them while she eats breakfast. And this is when Marion's book trouble starts. She is fixing her toast when …

Plop! She drops raspberry jam right on the book.

At first, Marion isn't worried; she has spilled on her own books lots of times. She calls her dog. He licks and licks and licks the page until it isn't sticky anymore. Actually, now it is kind of slimy, but the red stain is still there.

Marion imagines Mrs. Carlson's face frowning when she discovers the raspberry red stain on the beautiful book. She imagines Mrs. Carlson telling her she can never check out another book from the Media Center. She imagines never getting to be a librarian! What should she do?

She can't tell Mommy; Mommy doesn't like it when Marion brings books to the table. She can't tell Nana or Daddy either. They would want to know why she had the book on the breakfast table.

Marion thinks and thinks about how to get the stain out. Then she thinks about how she gets herself clean. This gives her a bright idea! She grabs the book and races to the bathroom. Maybe toothpaste will work! After all, toothpaste makes her teeth white and clean.

Marion spreads a thick line of toothpaste onto the raspberry red stain, then rubs it around. At first it looks whiter, but no, the raspberry stain is still there.

This stain is going to take something more, Marion thinks. She starts filling the bathtub. When Mommy knocks on the door and asks what Marion is doing, she truthfully says taking a bath and reading.

But the raspberry stain doesn't wash away in the bathtub, even when Marion adds bubble bath to the water.

Oh, what can Marion do? Then she remembers the washing machine and the new detergent that Mommy just bought. Marion read on the box that it is specially made to remove stains. Marion knows this will do the trick! It says on the box that it's guaranteed to work!

A short time later, Marion pulls the book from the washing machine and there is … nothing! The stain is gone, but so are the words and the pictures! The detergent washed everything away!

Oh no! Marion knows that she can't return this book to the Media Center. No one can ever read this book again. Then Marion has another idea. Maybe I can trade it for one of my books, she thinks.

First Marion pushes the book to the very back of her closet where no one will ever find it. Next she looks through her books to find one that she can take to school instead. Marion knows that the book she brings in will have to be a very good one. She carefully looks through each book, pretending that she is Mrs. Carlson.

The first book she chooses has some peanut butter on one of the pages. The next has a chocolate milk stain on two of the pages. The pages of another are dirty from the playground. Marion is surprised to see that every one of her books has dirty, torn, or bent pages. Is it possible, she wonders, that she doesn't take good care of her books?

With tears in her eyes, she goes to her closet, digs the book out of its hiding place, and goes to find Mommy.

Mommy and Daddy are disappointed with Marion. They tell her that she will have to return the ruined book to Mrs. Carlson. Marion will have to replace the ruined book.

On Sunday night Marion empties her piggy bank. She hopes that it will be enough to pay for the book. She also hopes that Mrs. Carlson will let her check out more books.

When Nana comes in to say good night, she reminds Marion of the good lesson she learned. Marion goes to sleep knowing she will never take her books to the breakfast table, out to play in the yard, or into the bathtub again.

When Marion brings the book back to the Media Center, she is very nervous. She holds the book up to Mrs. Carlson, who looks very sad. She gently takes the book from Marion's hands and holds it carefully. Then she asks Marion what happened.

As Marion explains, Mrs. Carlson listens. She asks Marion to explain what she will do differently the next time she checks out books from the Media Center.

Finally, Mrs. Carlson asks Marion if she would like to see the book hospital. Mrs. Carlson explains that the book hospital is where she and her staff work to clean and repair books that have been injured.

Before Marion leaves, Mrs. Carlson looks up the price of the book so that Marion can pay to replace it. She also gives Marion a Healthy Book bookmark to help her remember the right way to treat her books.

And of course, Marion finishes her visit by checking out two more books!

About Brook Berg and Marion the Hedgehog

Brook Berg is the District Media Specialist in Detroit Lakes, a small town in northern Minnesota. She spends her days at Detroit Lakes Middle School where she teaches students how to find the information and the books they need.

Marion was a real hedgehog who lived with Brook for many years. She often visited the Magelssen Elementary School library where students voted to name her Marion, after Marian the Librarian from *The Music Man*. Marion went to Hedgehog Heaven in 2001.

Brook and Marion liked to read books all year long, walk in Minnesota's north woods during the summer and spend lots of time in the Media Center reading with the students or helping them find good books.

Marion Hedgehog, the inspiration.